The Haunted House

and Other Spooky Poems and Tales

Edited by Vic Crume and Gladys Schwarcz

Illustrations by Gerry Contreras

SCHOLASTIC BOOK SERVICES

NEW YORK · TORONTO · LONDON · AUCKLAND · SYDNEY · TOKYO

ACKNOWLEDGMENTS

For reprint permission grateful acknowledgment is made to:

Mrs. Rowena Bennett for first five lines of "The Witch of Willowby Wood,"
© 1966 by Rowena Bennett. From *Creative Plays and Programs* by Rowena
Bennett, published by Plays, Inc., Boston, Mass.

Nathalia Crane for "Spooks" from *The Singing Crow and Other Poems* by Nathalia Crane, published by Albert and Charles Boni, Inc.

Vic Crume for "The Haunted House" by Vic Crume, © 1970 by Scholastic Maga-
zines, Inc.

Curtis Brown, Ltd., for "The Velvet Ribbon" from *Ghostly Fun* by Ann McGovern,
text © 1970 by Ann McGovern.

The Dial Press for "The Devil's Pocket," © 1968 by George Mendoza. From *The
Crack in the Wall and Other Terribly Weird Tales* by George Mendoza.

Doubleday & Co., Inc., for "The Bat," copyright 1938 by Theodore Roethke. From
The Collected Poems of Theodore Roethke.

E. P. Dutton & Co., Inc., for "The Old Wife and the Ghost" from *Blackbird in the
Lilac* by James Reeves. Published 1959 by E. P. Dutton & Co., Inc.; "The
Flattered Flying Fish" from *The Flattered Flying Fish and Other Poems* by
E. V. Rieu, © 1962 by E. V. Rieu.

Grosset & Dunlap, Inc., for "Voices" from *At the Top of My Voice and Other
Poems* by Felice Holman, © 1970 by Felice Holman. A W.W. Norton Book
published by Grosset & Dunlap, Inc.

ISBN: 0-590-09219-7

13 12 11 10 9 8   2 3 4 5 6/8

Printed in the U. S. A.   11

Contents

From Ghoulies and Ghosties,
And long-leggity Beasties,
And all things that go bump in the night,
Good Lord deliver us.

OLD CORNISH LITANY

The Haunted House

Not a window was broken
And the paint wasn't peeling,
  Not a porch step sagged —
  Yet, there was a feeling

That beyond the door
And into the hall
  This was the house of
  No one at all.

No one who breathed
Nor laughed, nor ate
  Nor said "I love,"
  Nor said "I hate."

Yet *something* walked
Along the stair
  Something that was
  And wasn't there.

And that is why weeds
On the path grow high,
  And even the moon
  Races fearfully by —

For *something* walks
Along the stair —
　Something that is
And isn't there.

VIC CRUME

A Skeleton Once in Khartoum

A skeleton once in Khartoum
Asked a spirit up into his room;
    They spent the whole night
    In the eeriest fight
As to which should be frightened of whom.

AUTHOR UNKNOWN

In Memory of Anna Hopewell

Here lies the body of Anna
Done to death by a banana.
It wasn't the fruit that laid her low
But the skin of the thing that made her go.

AUTHOR UNKNOWN

The Devil's Pocket

IT WAS an old, abandoned Vermont quarry, and the two brothers were forbidden to ever climb down into it or even go near it. A long time ago there had been a cave-in at the bottom of the quarry, and several men from the village had been trapped under tons of stone and slate. And they were never seen again.

"The stone swallowed them up!" their parents would warn the boys whenever they spoke of the quarry. Then they would be threatened with all kinds of punishments if they were ever caught near the quarry. And finally their father would look up from under his glasses, and in his deepest voice he would say, "It's the devil's pocket—don't ever throw a penny in it!"

And there were other stories still rumored in the village about the strange haunting echoes that filled the quarry late at night when the wind did not breathe.

But the more stories the boys heard about the quarry, the more fascinated they became with the devil's pocket.

"I'm not afraid," said Marty, looking down into the bottom of the quarry. "I'm going to throw a penny into it!"

"You better not!" cried Bruce. "We're not even supposed to be standing here." And he started to pull his younger brother away from the edge of the quarry.

"You're just afraid!" exclaimed Marty, taking an old, dull penny from his pocket and throwing it as far as he could into the quarry.

"You shouldn't have done that, Marty! You know what we were told!"

"Shhhhhhhh—listen."

"Ping! Pinggggggg!" echoed the quarry.

"CLINK! Pingggggggggggg!"

"Did you hear it? Did you hear? Did you hear my penny? C'mon, let's climb down—just once," cried Marty, suddenly breaking away from his brother.

"Marty—you come back here!"

But it was too late. Marty was already running down the side of the quarry.

"You're going to get it!" shouted Bruce as he chased after his brother.

And the devil's pocket echoed back:

"You're going to get it!

"GOING TO GET IT!

"GET IT!"

And before the echo died, both boys were standing side by side at the bottom of the quarry.

"Ooooooooooooooooooooooooo," cried Marty as loudly as he could.

"Ooooooooooooooooooooooo

"Ooooooooooooooo

"Ooooooooooo," echoed the devil's pocket back at them.

"Come on, Marty. Let's go home!"

And the devil's pocket repeated:

"Goooooooo hooooooome!

"GOOOOOOOO HOOOOOOOOOME!"

Ignoring his older brother, Marty began running around the bottom of the quarry, playing games with his echo, running and shouting until the quarry was filled with howls and screams and laughter.

Then all of a sudden Marty tripped over a rock, and for a moment the quarry was still.

"Now you've done it!" cried Bruce, running to help his brother.

"You've done it!

"YOU'VE DONE IT!

"DONE IT!"

And now the devil's pocket seemed to be mocking them.

"Look what I found!" Marty cried, jumping to his feet. "My penny! It's my penny!" And he held it up for his brother to see as he danced around and around with glee.

Then he shouted to the quarry, "I found my penny! I found my penny! I found my penny!"

"My penny!

"MY PENNY!

"MY PENNY!" echoed back the quarry.

"That's not your penny," said Bruce. "Look how shiny and new it is."

Marty looked down at the penny gleaming in the palm of his hand.

"It is so *my* penny." And he shouted back at the quarry, "It's *my* penny! It's *my* penny!"

But this time the devil's pocket did not echo back, and both boys stared at each other in the silence.

"I'm scared," Marty whimpered, stuffing the penny in his pocket. "Let's go home."

"Better not take it," Bruce whispered as he

carefully scanned the rocks and the sides of the quarry.

And the quarry echoed loudly:

"Better not take it!

"BETTER NOT TAKE IT!

"NOT TAKE IT!

"NOT TAKE IT!

"NOT TAKE IT!"

And the echo grew and swelled, repeating the same words over and over again as both boys scrambled up the side of the quarry and ran as fast as they could straight for home.

Before they went to bed, Marty placed the gleaming penny on the night table between their beds, and both boys took a long look at it before they finally fell asleep.

That night both boys had the same dream. They dreamed that the devil's pocket was calling them, calling them to give back the penny.

Perhaps it was only a dream, but when morning came, the two brothers found themselves huddled together in one bed — and the penny was gone!

GEORGE MENDOZA

The Old Wife and the Ghost

There was an old wife and she lived all alone
  In a cottage not far from Hitchin;
And one bright night, by the full moon light,
  Comes a ghost right into her kitchen.

About that kitchen neat and clean
  The ghost goes pottering round.
But the poor old wife is deaf as a boot
  And so hears never a sound.

The ghost blows up the kitchen fire,
  As bold as bold can be;
He helps himself from the larder shelf,
  But never a sound hears she.

He blows on his hands to make them warm,
  And whistles aloud "Whee-hee!"
But still as a sack the old soul lies
  And never a sound hears she.

From corner to corner he runs about,
  And into the cupboard he peeps;
He rattles the door and bumps on the floor,
  But still the old wife sleeps.

Jangle and bang go the pots and pans,
  As he throws them all around;
And the plates and mugs and dishes and jugs,
  He flings them all to the ground.

Madly the ghost tears up and down
  And screams like a storm at sea;
And at last the old wife stirs in her bed —
  And it's "Drat those mice," says she.

Then the first cock crows and morning shows
  And the troublesome ghost's away.
But oh! what a pickle the poor wife sees
  When she gets up next day.

"Them's tidy big mice," the old wife thinks,
  And off she goes to Hitchin,
And a tidy big cat she fetches back
  To keep the mice from her kitchen.

JAMES REEVES

Mother Goose
(Circa 2054)

Humpty Dumpty sat on the wall,
A non-electro-magnetic ball.
All the Super's polariscopes
Couldn't revitalize his isotopes.

IRENE SEKULA

The Superstitious Ghost

I'm such a quiet little ghost,
  Demure and inoffensive,
The other spirits say I'm most
  Absurdly apprehensive.

Through all the merry hours of night
  I'm uniformly cheerful;
I love the dark; but in the light,
  I own I'm rather fearful.

Each dawn I cower down in bed,
  In every brightness seeing,
That weird uncanny form of dread —
  An awful Human Being!

Of course I'm told they can't exist,
   That Nature would not let them:
But Willy Spook, the Humanist,
   Declares that he has met them!

He says they do not glide like us,
   But walk in eerie paces;
They're solid, not diaphanous,
   With arms! and legs!! and faces!!!

But should the dreadful day arrive
   When, starting up, I see one,
I'm sure 'twill scare me quite alive;
   And then—Oh, then I'll be one!

ARTHUR GUITERMAN

The Flattered Flying Fish
(The Shark and the Flying Fish)

Said the Shark to the Flying Fish over the phone:
"Will you join me tonight? I am dining alone.
Let me order a nice little dinner for two!
And come as you are, in your shimmering blue."

Said the Flying Fish: "Fancy remembering me,
And the dress I wore at the Porpoises' tea!"
"How could I forget?" said the Shark in his guile:
"I expect you at eight!" and rang off with a smile.

She has powdered her nose; she has put on her
    things;
She is off with one flap of her luminous wings.
O little one, lovely, light-hearted and vain.
The Moon will not shine on your beauty again!

E. V. RIEU

Ruth and Johnnie

Ruth and Johnnie,
  Side by side,
Went out for an
  Auto ride.
They hit a bump,
Ruth hit a tree,
And John kept going
  Ruthlessly.

AUTHOR UNKNOWN

It Isn't the Cough

It isn't the cough
That carries you off;
It's the coffin
They carry you off in.

AUTHOR UNKNOWN

Adventures of Isabel

Isabel met an enormous bear;
Isabel, Isabel, didn't care.
The bear was hungry, the bear was ravenous,
The bear's big mouth was cruel and cavernous.
The bear said, Isabel, glad to meet you,
How do, Isabel, now I'll eat you!
Isabel, Isabel, didn't worry,
Isabel didn't scream or scurry.
She washed her hands and she straightened
   her hair up,
Then Isabel quietly ate the bear up.

Once on a night as black as pitch
Isabel met a wicked old witch.
The witch's face was cross and wrinkled,
The witch's gums with teeth were sprinkled.
Ho, ho, Isabel! the old witch crowed,
I'll turn you into an ugly toad!
Isabel, Isabel, didn't worry,
Isabel didn't scream or scurry.
She showed no rage and she showed no rancor,
But she turned the witch into milk and drank her.

Isabel met a hideous giant,
Isabel continued self-reliant.
The giant was hairy, the giant was horrid,
He had one eye in the middle of his forehead.
Good morning, Isabel, the giant said,
I'll grind your bones to make my bread.
Isabel, Isabel, didn't worry,
Isabel didn't scream or scurry.
She nibbled the zwieback that she always fed off,
And when it was gone, she cut the giant's head off.

Isabel met a troublesome doctor,
He punched and he poked till he really
    shocked her.
The doctor's talk was of coughs and chills
And the doctor's satchel bulged with pills.
The doctor said unto Isabel,
Swallow this, it will make you well.
Isabel, Isabel, didn't worry,
Isabel didn't scream or scurry.
She took those pills from the pill-concocter,
And Isabel calmly cured the doctor.

OGDEN NASH

The Velvet Ribbon

ONCE there was a man who fell in love with a beautiful girl. And before the next full moon rose in the sky, they were wed.

To please her husband, the young wife wore a different gown each night. Sometimes she was dressed in yellow; other nights she wore red or blue or white. And she always wore a black velvet ribbon around her slender neck.

Day and night she wore that ribbon, and it was not long before her husband's curiosity got the better of him.

"Why do you always wear that ribbon?" he asked.

She smiled a strange smile and said not a word.

At last her husband got angry. And one night he shouted at his bride. "Take that ribbon off! I'm tired of looking at it."

"You will be sorry if I do," she replied. "So I won't."

Every morning at breakfast, the husband ordered his wife to remove the black velvet ribbon from around her neck. Every night at dinner he told her the same thing.

But every morning at breakfast and every night at dinner, all his wife would say was, "You'll be sorry if I do. So I won't."

A week passed. The husband no longer looked into his wife's eyes. He could only stare at that black velvet ribbon around her neck.

One night as his wife lay sleeping, he tiptoed to her sewing basket. He took out a pair of scissors.

Quickly and quietly, careful not to awaken her, he bent over his wife's bed

and

SNIP! went the scissors, and the velvet ribbon fell to the floor

and

SNAP! off came her head. It rolled onto the floor in the moonlight, wailing tearfully:

"I...told...you...you'd...be...s-o-r-r-y!"

ANN McGOVERN

Little Willie

Little Willie from his mirror
  Licked the mercury right off,
Thinking, in his childish error,
  It would cure the whooping cough.
At the funeral his mother
  Sadly said to Mrs. Brown:
" 'Twas a chilly day for Willie
When the mercury went down."

AUTHOR UNKNOWN

Jerry Jones

Six feet beneath
This funeral wreath
Is laid upon the shelf
One Jerry Jones,
Who dealt in bones,
And now he's bones himself.

AUTHOR UNKNOWN

The Cradle That Rocked by Itself

THERE was a raging storm at sea. The wind howled and lashed around many a snug house in many a little town up and down the coast of Maine. Many a ship at sea was in trouble that night, and some were never heard from again.

"I hear a baby crying out there," said a woman in one warm kitchen in one of those little towns. But the rest of the family said it was the wind howling, or seals, maybe, for a frightened baby seal often cries like a baby.

The woman said no. She knew in her heart it was a baby.

"How *could* it be?" said the others.

Nobody went out to look.

The next morning they found a cradle washed ashore, out of some ship. And they took it up to the house, for it was a good cradle. And they used it for every baby that came along, year after year.

But there was one strange thing about it: every time the wind blew a gale the cradle would rock by itself.

All by itself in the warm room, with the wind roaring outside, the cradle would rock just as if someone were sitting by it gently rocking a child.

This happened so often that the family got used to it. No harm ever came of it, and the baby liked it. So they just got used to it and didn't mind.

Then one time the woman's sister came to visit. As they were setting the table for supper one night, the sister glanced into the next room.

"Who is that woman rocking the cradle?" she said.

"Woman? That's no woman. The cradle rocks by itself."

"It is too a woman," said the sister. "She has long black hair and her face is white and sad, and she's sitting there rocking the cradle and bending over the baby."

Nobody else could see her. But the mother grabbed up her baby. And the next day they took the cradle outdoors and chopped it up for kindling wood.

And when the wood was burning in the fire, they could hear some baby crying—somewhere—crying and crying for its cradle.

But after that they never heard it again.

AS TOLD BY MARIA LEACH

The Wreck of the Hesperus

It was the schooner Hesperus,
  That sailed the wintry sea;
And the skipper had taken his little daughter,
  To bear him company.

Blue were her eyes as the fairy-flax,
  Her cheeks like the dawn of day,
And her bosom white as the hawthorn buds
  That ope in the month of May.

The skipper he stood beside the helm,
  His pipe was in his mouth,
And he watched how the veering flaw did blow
  The smoke now West, now South.

Then up and spake an old sailor,
  Had sailed the Spanish Main,
"I pray thee, put into yonder port,
  For I fear a hurricane.

"Last night, the moon had a golden ring,
  And to-night no moon we see!"
The skipper, he blew a whiff from his pipe,
  And a scornful laugh laughed he.

Colder and louder blew the wind,
  A gale from the Northeast,
The snow fell hissing in the brine,
  And the billows frothed like yeast.

Down came the storm, and smote amain
  The vessel in its strength;
She shuddered and paused, like a frighted steed,
  Then leaped her cable's length.

"Come hither! come hither! my little daughter,
  And do not tremble so;
For I can weather the roughest gale
  That ever wind did blow."

He wrapped her warm in his seaman's coat
   Against the stinging blast;
He cut a rope from a broken spar,
   And bound her to the mast.

"O father! I hear the church-bells ring,
   Oh say, what may it be?"
" 'Tis a fog-bell on a rock-bound coast!"—
   And he steered for the open sea.

"O father! I hear the sound of guns,
   Oh say, what may it be?"
"Some ship in distress, that cannot live
   In such an angry sea!"

"O father! I see a gleaming light,
   Oh say, what may it be?"
But the father answered never a word,
   A frozen corpse was he.

Lashed to the helm, all stiff and stark,
   With his face turned to the skies,
The lantern gleamed through the gleaming snow
   On his fixed and glassy eyes.

Then the maiden clasped her hands and prayed
   That saved she might be;
And she thought of Christ, who stilled the wave,
   On the Lake of Galilee.

And fast through the midnight dark and drear,
   Through the whistling sleet and snow,
Like a sheeted ghost, the vessel swept
   Towards the reef of Norman's Woe.

And ever the fitful gusts between
   A sound came from the land;
It was the sound of the trampling surf,
   On the rocks and the hard sea-sand.

The breakers were right beneath her bows,
   She drifted a dreary wreck,
And a whooping billow swept the crew
   Like icicles from her deck.

She struck where the white and fleecy waves
   Looked soft as carded wool,
But the cruel rocks, they gored her side
   Like the horns of an angry bull.

Her rattling shrouds, all sheathed in ice,
　　With the masts went by the board;
Like a vessel of glass, she stove and sank,
　　Ho! ho! the breakers roared!

At daybreak, on the bleak sea-beach,
　　A fisherman stood aghast,
To see the form of a maiden fair,
　　Lashed close to a drifting mast.

The salt sea was frozen on her breast,
   The salt tears in her eyes;
And he saw her hair, like the brown sea-weed,
   On the billows fall and rise.

Such was the wreck of the Hesperus,
   In the midnight and the snow!
Christ save us all from a death like this
   On the reef of Norman's Woe!

HENRY WADSWORTH LONGFELLOW

The Yarn of the "Nancy Bell"

" 'Twas in the good ship Nancy Bell
  That we sail'd to the Indian sea,
And there on a reef we come to grief,
  Which has often occurr'd to me.

"And pretty nigh all o' the crew was drown'd
  (There was seventy-seven o' soul);
And only ten of the Nancy's men
  Said 'Here!' to the muster-roll.

"There was me, and the cook, and the captain bold,
  And the mate of the Nancy brig,
And the bo'sun tight and a midshipmite,
  And the crew of the captain's gig.

"For a month we'd neither wittles nor drink,
  Till a-hungry we did feel,
So we draw'd a lot, and, accordin', shot
  The captain for our meal.

"The next lot fell to the Nancy's mate,
  And a delicate dish he made;
Then our appetite with the midshipmite
  We seven survivors stay'd.

"And then we murder'd the bo'sun tight,
  And he much resembled pig;
Then we wittled free, did the cook and me,
  On the crew of the captain's gig.

"Then only the cook and me was left,
  And the delicate question, 'Which
Of us two goes to the kettle?' arose,
  And we argued it out as sich.

"For I loved that cook as a brother, I did,
  And the cook he worshipp'd me;
But we'd both be blow'd if we'd either be stow'd
  In the other chap's hold, you see.

" 'I'll be eat if you dines off me,' says Tom.
  'Yes, that,' says I, 'you'll be.
I'm boil'd if I die, my friend,' quoth I;
  And 'Exactly so,' quoth he.

"Says he: 'Dear James, to murder me
  Were a foolish thing to do,
For don't you see that you can't cook *me*,
  While I can — and will — cook *you?*'

"So he boils the water, and takes the salt
  And the pepper in portions true
(Which he never forgot), and some chopp'd shallot,
  And some sage and parsley too.

" 'Come here,' says he, with a proper pride,
  Which his smiling features tell;
'Twill soothing be if I let you see
  How extremely nice you'll smell.'

"And he stirr'd it round and round and round,
  And he sniff'd at the foaming froth;
When I ups with his heels, and smothers his squeals
  In the scum of the boiling broth.

"And I eat that cook in a week or less,
  And as I eating be
The last of his chops, why I almost drops,
  For a wessel in sight I see.

"And I never larf, and I never smile,
  And I never lark nor play;
But I sit and croak, and a single joke
  I have — which is to say:

"Oh, I am a cook and a captain bold,
  And the mate of the Nancy brig,
And a bo'sun tight, and a midshipmite,
  And the crew of the captain's gig!"

WILLIAM SCHWENCK GILBERT

A Sea Dirge

Full fathom five thy father lies:
　Of his bones are coral made;
Those are pearls that were his eyes:
　Nothing of him that doth fade
But doth suffer a sea-change
Into something rich and strange.

FROM "THE TEMPEST"
BY WILLIAM SHAKESPEARE

The Ghost Catcher

Now this is a very old story. It is about a young barber who did not really want to be a barber. And it is about a ghost — two ghosts.

The young barber's name was Tom. Tom didn't like being a barber. He didn't like cutting men's hair or shaving their faces. He really wanted to be a farmer.

But Tom's father was a barber. And when Tom's father died, all he left his son was his bag of barber tools — razors, scissors, brushes, combs, and a mirror. So what could Tom do?

He tried to be a barber too. In those days, you had to do whatever your father did.

Well, Tom was a clever boy, but he wasn't a good barber. And after a while people stopped coming to him.

"He is not as good a barber as his father," they said.

"I'd rather be a farmer," Tom thought. "But if I have to be a barber, I will leave this town. I will go to the city where no one knows that my father was a better barber than I."

And so Tom picked up his bag of barber tools — razors, scissors, brushes, combs, and a mirror — and set off for the city.

Tom walked all morning and he walked all afternoon.

When night came, Tom sat under a willow tree to rest. The city was still a long way off, and Tom decided to spend the night under the willow tree. "Then I can start out fresh in the morning," he said to himself. Tom lay down on the ground and fell asleep at once.

As luck would have it, that very willow tree was haunted by a ghost.

Soon after Tom fell asleep, the ghost floated

down from the treetop crying, "BOOOOOOO!"

Tom woke up at once. "What a bad dream," he said to himself. "I dreamed this willow tree was haunted by a ghost."

"BOOOOOOOO!" cried the ghost again. Now he was right at Tom's ear. This was not a dream! Tom had to think fast.

"Don't you come close to me, ghost," Tom said quickly. "D-Do you know what I am? I-I'm a GHOST CATCHER! That's what I am! I catch ghosts and put them in my ghost bag."

And with that Tom opened his bag of barber tools and pulled up the mirror. "Here, let me show you one ghost I've caught tonight," he said. Tom held the mirror up to the ghost's face. "I think I'll put you in the bag to keep him company."

The ghost looked into the mirror — and what did he see? His own face, of course. But he didn't know that. He thought the barber really did have a ghost in the bag.

"Oh, please," begged the ghost, "don't put me in your ghost bag. I'll give you anything you want. Just let me go."

"Anything I want?" said Tom. "Then I want

a bag of gold. Maybe two bags of gold."

Zip! In a wink two bags of gold were at Tom's feet.

"Good enough," Tom said. "I promise not to put you in my bag this time. But remember, if you bother me again, into the ghost bag you go." As soon as Tom let the mirror fall back into the bag, the ghost was gone.

Tom never did go to the city. He took some of the gold the ghost had given him and he bought himself a farm. He bought cows and pigs and horses and chickens. Tom was a fine farmer. He didn't have to cut hair or shave faces anymore. But Tom kept his bag of barber tools — and that was very clever of him.

For, as luck would have it, the ghost met his

cousin one day and told him everything that had happened. At the end of his story, the cousin burst out laughing.

"Hoo, hoo, hoo," he laughed. "No man can catch a ghost. And there is no such thing as a ghost bag. You have been tricked."

"Well, go and see for yourself," the ghost said. "But don't blame me if that man puts you in his bag."

The cousin floated over to Tom's house and peeked through the window.

Tom was eating his supper. He felt a cold breeze and looked up. Another ghost! Tom ran to get his bag of tools. Quickly, he opened the bag and pulled up the mirror.

Then he held the mirror against the window and shouted "Come on in! I'll put you in the bag too!"

The cousin took one look at the ghost in the bag and floated off as fast as he could go.

From that time on Tom lived in peace. He was clever enough to keep his bag of barber tools handy, although he never had to use them again.

A TALE FROM INDIA
RETOLD BY E. B. CHANCE

The Great Auk's Ghost

The Great Auk's ghost rose on one leg,
Sighed thrice and three times winkt,
And turned and poached a phantom egg
And muttered, "I'm extinct."

RALPH HODGSON

Any Day Now

Johnny reading in his comic
Learned to handle the atomic.
Johnny blew us all to vapors.
What a lad for cutting capers!

DAVID McCORD

from *The Witch of Willowby Wood*

There once was a witch of Willowby Wood,
and a weird wild witch was she, with hair that was
  snarled
and hands that were gnarled, and a kickety, rickety
knee. She could jump, they say,
to the moon and back, but this I never did see.

ROWENA BENNETT

A Young Lady from Glitch

There was a young lady from Glitch
Who tried to turn into a witch.
  But she found that the most
  She could be was a ghost,
So she threw herself into a ditch.

TAMARA KITT

The Purist

I give you now Professor Twist,
A conscientious scientist.
Trustees exclaimed, "He never bungles."
And sent him off to distant jungles.
Camped on a tropic riverside,
One day he missed his loving bride,
She had, the guide informed him later,
Been eaten by an alligator.
Professor Twist could not but smile.
"You mean," he said, "a crocodile."

OGDEN NASH

The Kilkenny Cats

There wanst was two cats at Kilkenny,
Each thought there was one cat too many,
    So they quarrell'd and fit,
    They scratch'd and they bit,
    Till, excepting their nails,
    And the tips of their tails,
Instead of two cats, there warnt any.

AUTHOR UNKNOWN

Dust

Agatha Morley
All her life
Grumbled at dust
Like a good wife.

Dust on a table,
Dust on a chair,
Dust on a mantel
She couldn't bear.

She forgave faults
In man and child
But a dusty shelf
Would set her wild.

She bore with sin
Without protest,
But dust thoughts preyed
Upon her rest.

Agatha Morley
Is sleeping sound
Six feet under
The mouldy ground.

Six feet under
The earth she lies
With dust at her feet
And dust in her eyes.

SYDNEY KING RUSSELL

Windy Nights

Whenever the moon and stars are set,
  Whenever the wind is high,
All night long in the dark and wet,
  A man goes riding by.
Late in the night when the fires are out,
Why does he gallop and gallop about?

Whenever the trees are crying aloud,
  And ships are tossed at sea,
By, on the highway, low and loud,
  By at the gallop goes he.
By at the gallop he goes, and then
By he comes back at the gallop again.

ROBERT LOUIS STEVENSON

Voices

There are songs and sounds in stillness
In the quiet after dark,
Sounds within sounds,
Songs within songs.

There are rhythms in the quiet
And pulses in the night,
Beats within beats,
Drums within drums.

Something calling in the embers,
Something crying in the rocks,
And out beyond the darkness
There are voices in the stars.

FELICE HOLMAN

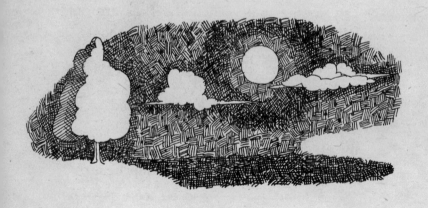

Winter Moon

How thin and sharp is the moon tonight!
How thin and sharp and ghostly white
Is the slim curved crook of the moon tonight!

LANGSTON HUGHES

November Night

Listen . . .
With faint dry sound,
Like steps of passing ghosts,
The leaves frost-crisped, break from the trees
And fall.

ADELAIDE CRAPSEY

The Erl-King

Who rides so late in a night so wild?
A father is riding with his child.
He clasps the boy close in his arm;
He holds him tightly, he keeps him warm.

"My son, you are trembling. What do you fear?"
"Look, father, the Erl-King! He's coming near!
With his crown and his shroud! Yes, that is he!"
"My son, it's only the mist you see."

"O lovely child, oh come with me,
Such games we'll play! So glad we'll be!
Such flowers to pick! Such sights to behold!
My mother will make you clothes of gold!"

"O father, my father, did you not hear
The Erl-King whispering in my ear?"
"Lie still, my child, lie quietly.
It's only the wind in the leaves of the tree."

"Dear boy, if you will come away,
My daughters will wait on you every day;
They'll give you the prettiest presents to keep;
They'll dance when you wake and they'll sing you
    asleep."

"My father! My father! Do you not see
The Erl-King's pale daughters waiting for me?"
"My son, my son, I see what you say —
The willow is waving its branches of gray."

"I love you — so come without fear or remorse.
And if you're not willing, I'll take you by force!"
"My father! My father! Tighten your hold!
The Erl-King has caught me—his fingers are cold!"

The father shudders. He spurs on his steed.
He carries the child with desperate speed.
He reaches the courtyard, and looks down with
    dread.
There in his arms the boy lies dead.

JOHANN WOLFGANG VON GOETHE
TRANSLATED BY LOUIS UNTERMEYER

Shadows Before Dawn
from *A Song of Sherwood*

Sherwood in the twilight, is Robin Hood awake?
Gray and ghostly shadows are gliding through the
brake;
Shadows of the dappled deer, dreaming of the
morn,
Dreaming of a shadowy man that winds a shadowy
horn.

Robin Hood is here again: all his merry thieves
Hear a ghostly bugle note shivering through the
leaves,
Calling as he used to call, faint and far away
In Sherwood, in Sherwood, about the break of
day.

ALFRED NOYES

from *Sir Roderic's Song*

When the night wind howls in the chimney cowls,
  and the bat in the moonlight flies,
And inky clouds, like funeral shrouds, sail over
  the midnight skies —
When the footpads quail at the night-bird's wail,
  and black dogs bay at the moon,
Then is the spectres' holiday — then is the ghosts'
  highnoon!

WILLIAM SCHWENCK GILBERT

The Bat

By day the bat is cousin to the mouse.
He likes the attic of an aging house.

His fingers make a hat about his head.
His pulse beat is so slow we think him dead.

He loops in crazy figures half the night
Among the trees that face the corner light.

But when he brushes up against a screen,
We are afraid of what our eyes have seen:

For something is amiss or out of place
When mice with wings can wear a human face.

THEODORE ROETHKE

The Listeners

"Is there anybody there?" said the Traveler,
  Knocking on the moonlit door;
And his horse in the silence champed the grasses
  Of the forest's ferny floor.
And a bird flew up out of the turret,
  Above the Traveler's head:
And he smote upon the door again a second time;
  "Is there anybody there?" he said.
But no one descended to the Traveler;
  No head from the leaf-fringed sill
Leaned over and looked into his gray eyes,
  Where he stood perplexed and still.
But only a host of phantom listeners
  That dwelt in the lone house then
Stood listening in the quiet of the moonlight
  To that voice from the world of men:
Stood thronging the faint moonbeams on the dark
  stair
  That goes down to the empty hall,
Hearkening in an air stirred and shaken
  By the lonely Traveler's call.

And he felt in his heart their strangeness,
  Their stillness answering his cry,
While his horse moved, cropping the dark turf,
  'Neath the starred and leafy sky;
For he suddenly smote on the door, even
  Louder, and lifted his head: —
"Tell them I came, and no one answered,
  That I kept my word," he said.
Never the least stir made the listeners,
  Though every word he spake
Fell echoing through the shadowiness of the still
    house
  From the one man left awake:
Aye, they heard his foot upon the stirrup,
  And the sound of iron on stone,
And how the silence surged softly backward,
  When the plunging hoofs were gone.

WALTER DE LA MARE

The Red Room
(edited and abridged)

"I CAN ASSURE YOU," said I, "that it will take a very real ghost to frighten me." And I stood up before the fire with my glass in my hand.

"It is your own choosing," said the man with the withered arm.

"Never a ghost have I seen as yet," said I.

The old woman sat staring hard into the fire, her pale eyes wide open. "Ay," she broke in, "you have lived and never seen the likes of this house." She swayed her head slowly from side to side. "Many things to see and sorrow for."

"Well," I said, "if I see anything tonight, I shall be so much the wiser. For I come to the business with an open mind."

"It's your own choosing," said the man.

I heard the sound of a stick and a shambling step in the passage outside, and the door creaked on its hinges as a second old man entered, more bent, more wrinkled, more aged even than the first. The old woman took no notice of his arrival, but remained with her eyes fixed steadily on the fire.

"If," said I, "you will show me to this haunted room of yours, I will make myself comfortable there."

The newcomer jerked his head back so suddenly that it startled me, but no one answered. I waited a minute, glancing from one to the other.

"If," I said a little louder, "if you will show me to this haunted room of yours, I will relieve you from the task of entertaining me."

"There's a candle on the slab outside the door," said the man with the withered arm, looking at my feet as he addressed me. "But if you go to the Red Room tonight —"

"This night of all nights!" said the old woman.

"—you go alone," he finished.

"Very well," I answered. "And which way do I go?"

"You go along the passage for a bit," said he, "until you come to a door, and through that is a spiral staircase, and halfway up that is a landing and another door. Go through that and down the long corridor to the end, and the Red Room is on your left, up the steps."

"And are you really going?" said the newcomer.

"This night of all nights!" said the old woman.

"It is what I came for," I said. At the door I turned and looked at them, and saw they were all close together, dark against the firelight, staring at me over their shoulders, with an intent expression on their ancient faces.

"Good night," I said, setting the door open.

"It's your own choosing," said the man with the withered arm.

I left the door wide open until the candle was well alight, and then I shut them in and walked down the chilly, echoing passage.

I must confess that the oddness of these three old people affected me. They seemed to belong to another age, an older age, an age when things were different from this of ours — an age of omens and witches and ghosts. But with an effort I sent such thoughts away.

The long, drafty passage was chilly and dusty, and my candle flared and made weird shadows. The echoes rang up and down the spiral staircase, and a shadow came sweeping up after me, and one fled before me into the darkness. I came to the landing and stopped there for a moment, listening to a rustling that I fancied I heard. Then, satisfied of the absolute silence, I pushed open the door and stood in the corridor.

The effect was scarcely what I expected, for the

moonlight, coming in by the great window on the grand staircase, picked out everything in vivid black shadow or silver. Everything was in its place — the house might have been deserted yesterday instead of eighteen months ago. I stood rigid for half a minute perhaps. Then I advanced in the moonlight.

The door to the Red Room and the steps up to it were in a shadowy corner. I moved my candle from side to side, in order to see clearly.

I entered, closed the door behind me at once, turned the key I found in the lock, and stood with the candle held aloft, surveying the scene of my vigil — the great Red Room of Lorraine Castle, in which the young duke had died. Or, rather, in which he had *begun* his dying, for he had opened the door and fallen headlong down the steps I had just climbed. And looking around that large shadowy room, with its shadowy window bays, its recesses and alcoves, one could well understand the legends that had sprouted in its black corners. My candle was a little tongue of flame in its vastness, that failed to pierce the opposite end of the room, and left an ocean of mystery and suggestion beyond its island of light.

I began to walk about the room, peering round each article of furniture. I pulled up the blinds and examined the fastenings of the windows before closing the shutters, leaned forward and looked up the blackness of the wide chimney, and tapped the dark oak paneling for any secret opening. There were two big mirrors in the room, each with a pair of candles, and on the mantelshelf, too, were more candles in china candlesticks. All these I lit one after the other. The fire was laid, and I lit it, and when it was burning well, I stood round with my back to it and regarded the room again. I had pulled up a chintz-covered armchair and a table, to form a kind of barricade before me. My examination had done me good, but I still found the darkness of the place, and its perfect stillness, too much for the imagination. The echoing of the stir and crackling of the fire was no sort of comfort to me. At last, to reassure myself, I walked with a candle into the shadow and satisfied myself that there was nothing real there. I stood that candle upon the floor of the alcove, and left it in that position.

By this time I was in a state of nervous tension. I was sure that nothing supernatural could happen.

Yet the reds and blacks of the room troubled me. Even with seven candles the place was merely dim. The one in the alcove flared in a draft, and the fire flickering kept the shadows stirring. I recalled the candles I had seen in the passage. With a slight effort, I walked out into the moonlight, carrying a candle and leaving the door open. Presently I returned with as many as ten. These I put in various knick-knacks of china and placed where the shadows were deepest, some on the floor, some in the windows, until at last my seventeen candles were so arranged that not an inch of the room but had the direct light of at least one of them. It occurred to me that when the ghost came, I could warn him not to trip over them. The room was now quite brightly illuminated. There was something very cheery in these streaming flames.

Even with that, however, my vigil weighed heavily upon me. It was after midnight when the candle in the alcove suddenly went out, and the black shadow sprang back to its place. I did not see the candle go out. I simply turned and saw that the darkness was there, as one might start and see the unexpected presence of a stranger. And, taking the matches from the table, I walked across the room to relight the corner again. My first match would not strike, and as I succeeded with the second, something seemed to blink on the wall before me. I turned my head and saw that the two candles on the little table by the fireplace were out.

"Odd!" I said. "Did I do that?"

I walked back, relit one, and as I did so, I saw the candle in the right of one of the mirrors wink and go right out, and almost immediately its companion followed it. There was no mistake about it. The flame vanished, as if the wicks had been suddenly nipped between a finger and a thumb, leaving the wick neither glowing nor smoking, but black. While I stood gaping, the candle at the foot of the bed went out, and the shadows seemed to take another step toward me.

"This won't do!" said I, and first one and then another candle on the mantelshelf followed.

"What's up?" I cried, with a queer high note getting into my voice somehow. At that the candle on the wardrobe went out, and the one I had relit in the alcove followed.

"Steady on!" I said. "These candles are

wanted." I scratched away at a match for the mantel candlesticks. My hands trembled so much that twice I missed the rough paper of the matchbox. As the mantel emerged from darkness again, two candles in the window went out. But with the same match I also relit the large mirror candles, and those on the floor near the doorway. Then four lights vanished in different corners of the room, and I struck another match in quivering haste, and stood hesitating where to take it.

As I stood undecided, an invisible hand seemed to sweep out the two candles on the table. With a cry of terror I dashed at the alcove, then into the corner, and then into the window, relighting three, as two more vanished by the fireplace. Then, seeing a better way, I caught up the bedroom candlestick. With this I avoided the delay of striking matches; but for all that, the shadows I feared returned, and crept in upon me. Now and then one returned for a minute, and was lost again. I was now almost frantic with the horror of coming darkness and my self-possession deserted me. I leaped panting from candle to candle, in a vain struggle against the advance of that shadow.

I bruised myself on the thigh against the table. I sent a chair headlong, I stumbled and fell and whisked the cloth from the table in my fall. My candle rolled away from me and I snatched another as I rose. Abruptly this was blown out, as I swung it off the table, by the wind of my sudden movement. Immediately the two remaining candles followed. But there was light still in the room, a red light that staved off the shadows from me. The fire! Of course, I could thrust my candle between the grate bars and relight it!

I turned to where the flames were dancing between the glowing coals and splashing red reflections upon the furniture, made two steps toward the grate, and the flames dwindled and vanished. The candle fell from my hand. I flung out my arms and lifting up my voice, screamed with all my might — once, twice, thrice. Then I think I must have staggered to my feet. I know I thought suddenly of the moonlit corridor, and, with my head bowed and my arms over my face, made a run for the door.

But I had forgotten the exact position of the door, and struck myself heavily against the corner of the bed. I staggered back, turned, and was

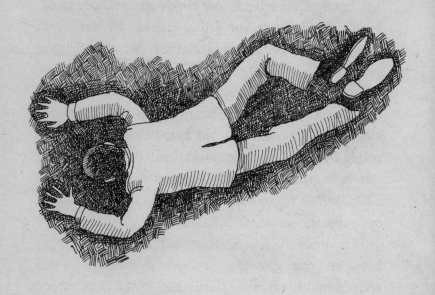

either struck or struck myself against some other bulky furniture. I have a memory of battering myself to and fro in the darkness, and of a heavy blow at last upon my forehead and a horrible sensation of falling that lasted an age. And then I remember no more.

I opened my eyes in daylight. My head was roughly bandaged, and the man with the withered arm was watching my face. I looked about me, trying to remember what had happened, and for a space I could not recollect. I turned to the corner, and saw the old woman pouring out some drops of medicine. "Where am I?" I asked. "I seem to remember you, and yet I cannot remember who you are."

They told me then, and I heard of the haunted Red Room as one who hears a tale. "We found you at dawn," said the old man, "and there was blood on your forehead and lips."

It was very slowly I recovered my memory of my experience. "You believe now," said the old man, "that the room is haunted?"

"Yes," said I. "The room is haunted."

"And you have seen it. And we, who have lived here all our lives, have never set eyes upon it. Because we have never dared. . . . Tell us, is it truly the old earl who —"

"No," said I, "it is not."

"I told you so," said the old lady, with the glass in her hand. "It is his poor young countess who was frightened —"

"It is not," I said. "There is neither ghost of earl nor ghost of countess in that room, there is no ghost there at all — but worse, far worse."

"Well?" they said.

"The worst of all the things that haunt poor

mortal man," said I. "*Fear!* Fear that will not have light nor sound, that will not bear with reason, that deafens and darkens and overwhelms. It followed me through the corridor, it fought against me in the room —"

I stopped abruptly. There was a moment of silence. Then the old man sighed and spoke. "I knew that was it. A Power of Darkness. It lurks there always. You can feel it even in the daytime, even of a bright summer's day, in the hangings, in the curtains, keeping behind you however you face about. In the dusk it creeps along the corridor and follows you, so that you dare not turn. There is Fear in that room—dark Fear. And there will be—so long as this house of sin endures."

H. G. WELLS

The Two Old Women of Mumbling Hill

The two old trees on Mumbling Hill,
They whisper and chatter and never keep still.
What do they say as they lean together
In rain or sunshine or windy weather?

There were two old women lived near the hill,
And they used to gossip as women will
Of friends and neighbors, houses and shops,
Weather and trouble and clothes and crops.

And one sad winter they both took ill,
The two old women of Mumbling Hill.
They were bent and feeble and wasted away
And both of them died on the selfsame day.

Now the ghosts of the women of Mumbling Hill,
They started to call out loud and shrill,
"Where are the tales we used to tell,
And where is the talking we loved so well?"

Side by side stood the ghosts until
They both took root on Mumbling Hill;
And they turned to trees, and they slowly grew,
Summer and winter the long years through.

In winter the bare boughs creaked and cried,
In summer the green leaves whispered and sighed;
And still they talk of fine and rain,
Storm and sunshine, comfort and pain.

The two old trees of Mumbling Hill,
They whisper and chatter and never keep still.
What do they say as they lean together
In rain or sunshine or windy weather?

JAMES REEVES

Spooks

Oh, I went down to Framingham
    To sit on a graveyard wall;
"If there be spooks," I said to myself,
    "I shall see them, one and all."

I hugged the knee to still the heart,
    My gaze on a tomb 'neath a tree.
Down in the village the clock struck nine,
    But never a ghost did I see.

A boy passed by, and his hair was red;
    He paused by a sunken mound.
"How goes it with all the ghosts?" said he.
    "Have you heard any walking around?"

Now the taunt was the sign of a boy's disdain
  For the study I did pursue.
So I took the hour to teach that lad
  Of the things unseen but true.

And suddenly a bat swung by,
  Two cats began to bawl,
And that red-haired boy walked off in haste
  When I needed him most of all.

I lost a slipper as I fled —
  I bumped against a post;
But nevertheless I knew I'd won
  The secret of raising a ghost.

And the method is this — at least for a miss —
  You must sit on a graveyard wall,
And talk of the things you never have seen,
  And you'll see them, one and all.

NATHALIA CRANE